If YOU Give a ~~Rex~~ a Bone

By Tim Myers

Illustrated by
Anisa Claire Hovemann

DAWN Publications

If you give a T. rex a bone, he's gonna be mad.

T. rex, you see, is incorrigibly carnivorous and usually quite hungry. He won't consider a bare bone proper nourishment.

So if you give a T. rex a bone—get ready to run.
But if you run from a T. rex, you may be in trouble.
They like to chase things; it's what they do.
Try dodging into the underbrush
where he can't see you.
After a couple hours he'll
probably stop looking.

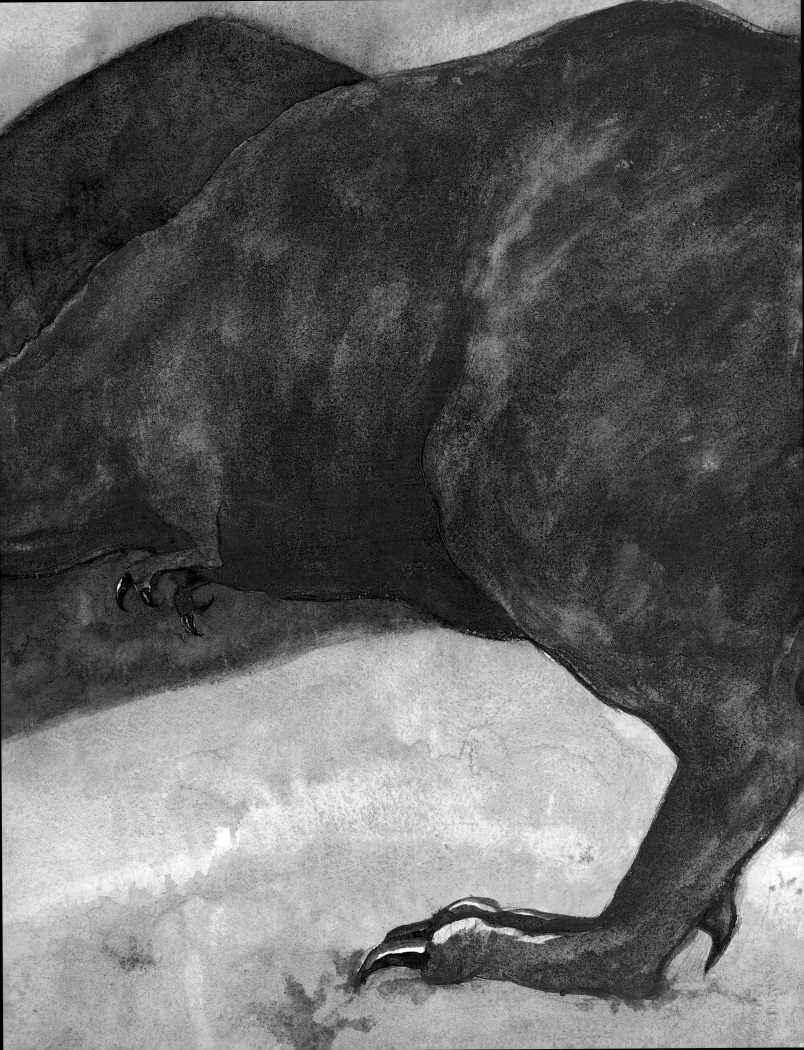

But if
you're hiding
in the underbrush,
you might encounter a
Dimetrodon—that cute,
low-slung guy with the big
fin on his back. Only he's also
got knife-like teeth and
super-powerful jaws.
And—surprise!—he's a
meat-eater too.

So if you encounter a *Dimetrodon*,
it's best to skip the introductions and
take off—quickly.
Maybe into a nearby bay.

But if you slip into
a bay, you may attract a
Kronosaurus. There you are, bobbing
around like a tasty fish, and suddenly this toothy
guy snuggles up to you. Oh yeah—he's 42 feet long.

So if you attract a kronosaur, you may want to swim
rapidly out of the bay into a river too small for
him to follow.

But if you swim into a river, you might be
spotted by a *Dakosaurus*.

See, the females come to shallow rivers to lay eggs.
Heck—they're only 20 feet long. Just try not to look
at those barracuda-style teeth.

So if you're spotted by a dakosaur, don't stick around for the
baby shower. Get out of the river and climb a ridge that rises
above the jungle, where you can catch your breath.

But if you climb a ridge, you might be
dived at by a **Quetzalcoatlus**.

If you're dived at by a *Quetzalcoatlus*,
the outcome could be unpleasant.
He's basically the size of a small plane.
And he may think you're the best thing
on the menu. So you better fling
yourself into the open ocean.

But if you fling
yourself into the
ocean, you may be knocked
silly by a **Shonisaurus**.

A shonisaur can be 46 feet
long and weigh 80,000
pounds. That's a lot of critter.
And a lot of hungry. So if you don't
want to rent space in his house-sized
belly—permanently—you should swim
for the beach.

But if you're on the beach, you might happen upon a **Dilophosaurus**. She's got pretty markings and a lovely crest—but that same serious meat habit, and huge claws for silverware. So you should make a beeline for the bushes again, hoping she doesn't see you.

But if you're in the bushes, a **Hylonomus** might slip into your backpack. No problem, you say—he's only a foot long. Well, yeah. But he's a fierce hunter—and he's even got teeth in his throat! Try fishing that snarly little dude up out of your pack. So you better climb a tree.

But if you're up a tree, you may get knocked out of it by a ***Brachiosaurus***.

She's no meat-eater, but she's 60 feet tall. And she loves chewing stuff high in trees. Her head's as big as you are—and I don't think she's an especially careful eater.
So you better climb down.

But if you climb down, you may come to a marsh
and be greeted by a **Deinosuchus**.

He'll look familiar—just a crocodile, after all. But he's
40 feet long, with another inviting mouthful of
teeth, and a head as big as a small car.
So if you don't want to stay for dinner,
better hurry to firmer ground.

But if you're
on firmer ground, you might
spark the interest of a **Velociraptor**.

She's only as big as a coyote, and she has a
slightly bird-like look to her. But this is no
canary. She runs like the wind and has
sharp teeth, slashing hand-claws,
and extra-large foot-claws like
grappling hooks. Oh, and she
and her friends hunt in packs.
So you better head for the woods.

But if you're in the woods, you might disturb a **Triceratops**.

She's a plant-eater, but she gets mad pretty quick; with all those meat-eaters around, you can hardly blame her! And if she charges with that huge horn and those spikes, she could make you look like Swiss cheese. So you best get out the woods, Red Riding Hood.

But when you
emerge from the
trees—what luck!
Right in front of you
is the ENORMOUS
skeleton of what used to be
a **Seismosaurus**! It's 145 feet long and
crowded with individual bones—the perfect
place to hang out and feel safe!

But if you're hanging out inside a seismosaur
skeleton, you might get unexpected company.
Did I mention that *T. rex* is also a scavenger?
That means he's likely to poke around old bones
like these—and he's certainly strong enough
to break through them.

So there you are, back to giving a *T. rex* a bone.
And we've already discussed that.

Tim Talks Dinos

When I think of ancient reptiles, I'm just blown away. How could such fascinating creatures actually exist? But the many fossils we've found all over the world show they were really here. Which is just so **cool**!

I didn't make anything up for this book; it's all based on science. But one part isn't accurate. I wanted to show the great variety of ancient reptiles, so I put animals from different time periods together, when many of them actually died out millions of years apart. You should realize too that some of what we know about these species is fact, because we have direct evidence. Fossilized bones, for example, show us the animals' sizes. Even some behavior—like moving in herds or caring for eggs—can be proven by fossils. But other things, like other behaviors or skin color, come from experts' ideas of what's likely to be true but isn't certain.

Oh, and one more thing: you **couldn't** have been there. These guys were all extinct for at least 65 million years before humans showed up. Reassuring, isn't it? But let me tell you a little more about the individual species.

Dimetrodon (die-ME-tro-don) wasn't actually a dinosaur but a pelycosaur. His fin may have worked to cool or warm him when he needed it. But don't be fooled by his grin: this 10-foot-long guy was one of the biggest meat-eaters of his day, with long stabbing fangs in the front of his mouth and slashing teeth in the back. To the animals of his time, he was *T. rex*!

If you saw a ***Kronosaurus*** (KRON-ah-sawr-us) today, you'd probably call it a monster. Kronosaurs weren't dinosaurs either, but swimming reptiles called pliosaurs—and they were huge! Their heads could be eight and a half feet long—twice as big as *T. rex's*—and since they're named after the Greek god who ate his own children, you can guess what kind of "personality" they had. This predator was two times as long as the longest crocs today, and ten times heavier—and with 11-inch teeth!

Fossils of **dakosaurs** (DAK-ah-sawrz) discovered in Argentina led scientists to nickname this creature "Godzilla." It was a sea-going crocodile, only much bigger than most of the huge sea crocs of that time—and with a mouth like *T. rex*. Dakosaurs weren't afraid of other reptiles like ichthyosaurs and long-necked plesiosaurs, or sharks—because they ATE those dudes!

When scientists first found fossils of ***Quetzalcoatlus***, (ket-SAL-ko-AT-lus) they thought there was some mistake—it was just too big! The wingspan of this flying reptile could reach 40 feet. Using its dagger-shaped beak, it probably caught and ate fish like modern seabirds do.

The ***Shonisaurus*** (SHON-ah-sawr-us) is one of my favorites—it's just so enormous and weird! Shonisaurs are icthyosaurs, air-breathing marine reptiles. They had long thin snouts but gigantic bellies. When Nevada miners found a skeleton in the 1800's, they used its vertebrae bones for dinner plates! But that's nothing; a new fossil has been found in Canada—which is longer than a sperm whale!

You may remember the ***Dilophosaurus*** (die-LOF-ah-sawr-us) from *Jurassic Park*. There's actually no evidence that dilophosaurs spit poison. But we know they could reach 20 feet, weigh up to 1,000 pounds, and were fast and agile. And they might have hunted in packs. We don't need any poison-spitting in order to respect this guy.

Little ***Hylonomus*** (high-LA-na-mus) may not seem such a big deal. But he's possibly the first of all the reptiles—which means he was sort of the granddaddy of all the others! And he was equipped to deal with predators like giant dragonflies and meat-eating amphibians, so he's pretty cool too.

You've probably heard of ***Brachiosaurus***. (BRAK-e-ah-sawr-us) But did you know that some think she could reach up as high as 53 feet? That she had claws on her feet? That walking herds of brachiosaurs tore up the ground several yards well below the surface? Other dinosaurs have been discovered that seem to be bigger, but *Brachiosaurus* was so impressive one version of it is named *Giraffatitan*.

Deinosuchus (dye-no-SUE-kus) is another nightmare creature, an early, armor-plated crocodile that hunted—dinosaurs! Dino fossils show *Deinosuchus* teeth marks on them. The largest *Deinosuchus* were the size of *T. rex*. Imagine a 40-foot-long crocodile with a jaw six feet long, just lying around half-submerged in a swamp. Whoa.

Velociraptor (va-LOHS-ah-RAP-tor) is now a movie star—though she was actually only about as big as a coyote and was covered with feathers. But she did have that huge sickle-like claw on each foot, and may have run 40 miles per hour. One skeleton was found in a death-grip with a *Protoceratops* (a dinosaur like *Triceratops*), with its claw in the *Proto's* throat while the *Proto* was biting its arm. You've got to hand it to the raptor—she's one tough customer.

Triceratops (tri-SER-ah-tops) is my favorite. One of the last non-bird dinosaurs to become extinct, it had a bone frill around its head and horns as long as hockey sticks. Fossils have been found with *Tyrannosaurus* bite marks on them; one even had a broken horn that healed over. So *Triceratops*, it seems, could take care of itself in a dangerous world.

And the ***Seismosaurus*** (SIZE-ma-sawr-us)— it's GI-NORMOUS! In 1979, two hikers accidentally found a fossilized tail in New Mexico. It took paleontologists many years to excavate the full specimen. *Seismosaurus* isn't the biggest dinosaur, as we once thought; *Argentinosaurus* is the current champ. But with length estimates from 135 to 165 feet, Seismo was as long as half a football field. Would have made a heck of a water-slide, eh?

And what can I say about ***Tyrannosaurus rex*** (ti-RAN-ah-SAW-rus)? He's the most famous of all, even if he's no longer the biggest meat-eater. His teeth were the size of bananas. His huge strides could cover a LOT of ground. His skull shows he could tear out 500 pounds of meat in one bite. Even those puny arms were 10 times stronger than the strongest human's. All in all, he deserves to be called "Your Majesty." From a safe distance, of course.

But that's not all, folks! Because paleontologists are still out there hunting, and new species of ancient reptiles are being discovered, on the average, once every seven weeks. So stay tuned!

By the way, scientists italicize ancient reptile names that show genus or species. However, they do not italicize less formal names or names from more general categories. For example: *Brachiosaurus* and brachiosaur.

Dino Fun

Why not make your own ancient reptile flashcards? How about writing a story or play about "a day in the life" of a meat-eater, or a prey animal, or a young ancient reptile? You could use books to play a game of "What Ancient Reptile Am I?" with your friends, who have to guess from your description. You could even invent a new ancient reptile, a predator, and have your friend invent a prey animal who's evolved to protect itself. How about using sticks to make a "fossil," burying them scattered in the dirt, then having your friend dig them up and reassemble the ancient reptile? Or you could ask your grown-ups to take you to a museum, or even a dig.

And of course you can always read the many wonderful books and articles about these astounding animals. That's what I did. Good hunting!

Some great Dino books and websites

One of my favorite books is *A Gallery of Dinosaurs and Other Early Reptiles* (1989) by David Peters. It has beautiful realistic paintings that show the size of these amazing animals compared to kids!

Chased by Sea Monsters (2004) by Marven and James shows computer-graphic animals with real people in actual photos—scary and fun.

Dinosaur encyclopedias are great for looking up particular animals. Two especially good ones are *National Geographic Dinosaurs* (2001) by Paul Barrett and The *Concise Dinosaur Dictionary* (2004) by David Burnie.

The I Dig Dinosaurs books (2002) feature "rocks" from which young paleontologists can chip out dinosaur "bones."

Uncover T. Rex (2003) by Schatz, Keitzmueller and Bonadonna is built around a 3-D tyrannosaurus body with page-layers revealing skeleton, organs, etc.

Encyclopedia Prehistorica Dinosaurs: The Definitive Pop-Up (2005) offers superb visuals designed by paper-engineering masters Subuda and Reinhart.

The American Museum of Natural History has an awesome website at www.amnh.org. Kids: click on "Ology" and then "paleontology" for all kinds of stuff to do. Teachers: click on "Resources for Learning" and then on "paleontology."

The University of California Museum of Paleontology site, www.ucmp.berkeley.edu, is superb, though for advanced learners.

I also love the "Walking with Dinosaurs" site (from the TV show of the same name) at www.abc.net.au/dinosaurs.

Another fabulous website is www.oceansofkansas.com, which features fossils from the ancient sea that used to cover much of the American West and Midwest. This is a serious paleontology site, but even young explorers can simply click on the many links to various animals, questions, etc., and see fantastic pictures and photos.

Tim Myers is a writer who is inspired by his own life experiences. Once he was on a safari in Africa and was charged by a rhino. Once the jeep got stuck and hungry hyenas started circling. Once on a California beach he and his family found whale bones. And once upon a time his two boys were dinosaur buffs. Put it all together, add some imagination, and you get something like *If You Give a T-Rex a Bone*. Tim is also a storyteller and a lecturer at Santa Clara University in California.

Even as a very young artist, dinosaurs caught the attention of **Anisa Claire Hovemann**. When only three years old, she took colorful chunks of play putty and shaped them into remarkably lifelike dinosaurs. Years later she graduated with a degree in fine arts from the Maryland Institute College of Art. It was with delight that Anisa returned to the subject of dinosaurs for this project—this time using watercolor as her medium. She also illustrated *Eliza and the Dragonfly*, which was named "Best Picture Book" by the International Reading Association and "Outstanding Science Trade Book" by the Children's Book Council and the National Science Teacher Association. Anisa also teaches yoga and is a student of massage therapy.

OTHER "CREATIVE NON-FICTION" BOOKS FROM DAWN PUBLICATIONS THAT ENCOURAGE APPRECIATION FOR NATURE

Also illustrated by Anisa Claire Hovemann

Eliza and the Dragonfly by Susie Caldwell Rinehart, illustrated by Anisa Claire Hovemann. Almost despite herself, Eliza becomes entranced by the "awful" dragonfly nymph—and before long, both of them are transformed. Declared "Best Picture Book" for 2005 by the International Reading Association.

The Web at Dragonfly Pond by Brian "Fox" Ellis, illustrated by Michael S. Maydak. Fishing with father becomes a life-long memory of how the web of life at the pond connects us all.

Over in the Jungle: a Rainforest Rhyme and *Over in the Ocean: In a Coral Reef* by Marianne Berkes, illustrated by Jeanette Canyon. Stunning clay art accompanies delightful lyrics based on the classic tune of "Over in the Meadow."

The Habitat Series by Anthony Fredericks, illustrated by Jennifer DiRubbio, features creature-communities, seen as part of their own unique neighborhood.
  Under One Rock: Bugs, Slugs and other Ughs
  In One Tidepool: Crabs, Snails and Salty Tails
  Around One Cactus: Owls, Bats and Leaping Rats
  Near One Cattail: Turtles, Logs and Leaping Frogs
  On One Flower: Butterflies, Ticks and a few more Icks.

River Song by Steve Van Zandt, illustrated by Katherine Zecca with CD. Rivers make beautiful music - and here it is joined by children's musical ensemble, the Banana Slug String Band celebrating rivers as a fascinating, ever-changing source of life and joy.

If You Were My Baby: A Wildlife Lullaby by Fran Hodgkins, illustrated by Laura Bryant. Here is a unique blend of love song and non-fiction celebrating the care that exists between the parents and offspring of many species.

Stickeen: John Muir and the Brave Little Dog as retold by Donnell Rubay, illustrated by Chrisopher Canyon. *Stickeen* is the classic story of John Muir's true adventure with a little dog on an Alaskan glacier. The trial they go through transformed their relationship and gave Muir a "window" through which he could see into the heart of the animal kingdom.

Dedications

To Chuck Nolan and Terry Mallen, for their magnificent
friendship-and for sharing with me their immense
pleasure in knowledge. - TM

For Grandma and Grandpa Joy and Herman and
Grandma and Grandad Rita and Everett, with all my love. - ACH

Copyright © 2007 Timothy Joseph Myers

Illustration copyright © 2007 Anisa Claire Hovemann

A Sharing Nature With Children Book

Library of Congress Cataloging-in-Publication Data

Myers, Tim.
  If you give a T-rex a bone / by Tim Myers ; illustrated by Anisa Claire
Hovemann. -- 1st ed.
    p. cm.
  "A sharing nature with children book."
  Includes bibliographical references.
  Summary:"Dinosaurs and other ancient reptiles appear in their ancient
habitats as if witnessed by a modern day child. Includes information about
the animals and resources for additional learning"--Provided by publisher.
  ISBN 978-1-58469-097-9 (hardback) -- ISBN 978-1-58469-098-6 (pbk.)
  1. Reptiles, Fossil--Juvenile literature. 2. Dinosaurs--Juvenile
literature. I. Hovemann, Anisa Claire, ill. II. Title.
  QE861.5.M94 2007
  567.9--dc22

                              2007008332

Printed in China

10 9 8 7 6 5 4 3 2 1

First Edition

Design and computer production by Patty Arnold, Menagerie Design and Publishing

Dawn Publications

12402 Bitney Springs Road
Nevada City, CA 95959
530-274-7775
nature@dawnpub.com

Dawn Publications is dedicated to inspiring in children a deeper understanding and appreciation for all life on Earth. To review our titles or to order, please visit us at www.dawnpub.com, or call 800-545-7475.